10 Minute Tales

Everything's **ROSIE**

Raggles the Reporter

EGMONT
We bring stories to life

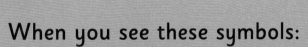

When you see these symbols:

Read aloud
Read aloud to
your child.

Read alone
Support your child
as they read alone.

Read along
Read along with
your child.

FSC
www.fsc.org
MIX
Paper from
responsible sources
FSC® C018306

Egmont is passionate about helping to preserve the world's remaining ancient forests.
We only use paper from legal and sustainable forest sources.

This book is made from paper certified by the Forestry Stewardship Council® (FSC®),
an organisation dedicated to promoting responsible management of forest resources.
For more information on the FSC®, please visit www.fsc.org. To learn more about
Egmont's sustainable paper policy, please visit www.egmont.co.uk/ethical

Read aloud   **Read along**

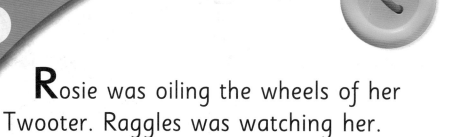

Rosie was oiling the wheels of her
Twooter. Raggles was watching her.
He was holding a little notepad and a pencil.

"Um. Do you like your Twooter, Rosie?" Raggles
asked.

"Of course I do!" laughed Rosie.

Raggles scribbled Rosie's answer in his notepad and
then smiled proudly.

"Today I'm Raggles the Reporter!" he announced.
"And I'm writing my very own newspaper."

Read alone

Raggles asks Rosie lots of questions.
He is being a newspaper reporter.

"**H**ow's this for my first story?" continued Raggles, "Rosie oils Twooter ... And it's faster than ever!"

"Well, it's very nice," said Rosie, kindly, "but it's not very exciting."

Raggles nodded. Rosie was right, he needed better stories for his newspaper to be a success.

"Just follow your nose," Rosie advised. "You'll soon find a story everyone wants to read!"

Raggles reads Rosie his first story, but it's too dull. He needs to find better stories.

Read aloud   Read along

Raggles set off to find some better stories. He saw Holly by Big Bear's apple tree.

Hanging from the tree was a juicy red apple. Holly stretched up and picked the apple.

"Big Bear is in for a big surprise!" she said as she ran away.

Raggles quickly scribbled down the story:

*Big Bear in for nasty surprise ...
Holly takes his apple!*

Read alone

Raggles sees Holly pick Big Bear's apple. He writes a story saying Big Bear is in for a shock.

Read aloud   Read along

Meanwhile, Bluebird was practising her magic. She was using a special spell to move her nest into a new tree, but the magic wasn't working!

"Come on, nest," squawked Bluebird, crossly. "Get up there, into that tree."

But the nest didn't move.

"Unhelpful nest," Bluebird muttered, "and this tree is silly!"

She stomped away in a huff.

Read alone

Bluebird is cross! Her magic spell doesn't lift her nest into the tree. She calls the tree silly.

Raggles was watching from behind a bush.

"Bluebird says trees are silly," repeated Raggles, "Now that's a brilliant story!

Raggles scribbled the story into his notepad and smiled.

"Rosie was right," he thought. "I just have to follow my nose and I find amazing stories."

He set off to find his next big scoop.

Raggles hears Bluebird call the tree silly.
He thinks it is a good story for his newspaper.

Read alone

Read aloud   Read along

At the bottom of Oakley's Hill, Raggles saw Will.

Will had a football. He placed the ball carefully on the ground. He then took a big run-up and kicked the ball up the hill. It bashed Oakley on the nose!

"Ouch!" cried Oakley.

"Ha, ha!" yelled Will as he ran away from the hill. "Nice one!"

Will has a football. He kicks the ball and it hits Oakley on the nose.

Read aloud   Read along

Raggles scribbled down another story: *Will kicks ball at Oakley ... then runs away laughing!*

He shut his notepad. He had enough stories for a whole newspaper now! He hurried away to write it.

Just then, Will came running back. He'd been to fetch the ball.

"Great save, Oakley!" he shouted.

"Thank you," chuckled Oakley, cheerfully.

They were playing football together!

Raggles writes a story about Will kicking
a ball at Oakley. But it was just a game!

Read alone

Read aloud Read along

Raggles was running to the Playhouse to write his newspaper when he bumped into Rosie.

"Did you get any good stories?" Rosie asked.

"A whole newspaper's worth!" replied Raggles, smiling happily.

Rosie wanted to read the stories straight away, but Raggles said she would have to wait until the newspaper was written.

"It'll be a surprise!" said Raggles.

Rosie wants to read the stories. Raggles says
she must wait until the newspaper is finished.

Read alone

Read aloud   Read along

Back at the Playhouse, Raggles
rushed inside to write his newspaper.
He was busy for a very long time, but
eventually he came back out, proudly waving
the finished copies.

Rosie and Raggles jumped onto the Twooter and
went to deliver the newspapers. Raggles threw a
copy to everyone they passed.

Soon, everyone was
reading the news!

Read alone

Soon the newspaper is ready.
Everyone is reading it.

Read aloud   Read along

While Oakley was reading the newspaper, Rosie and Raggles rested in the shade of his branches.

Oakley frowned as he read. "Bluebird says trees are silly," he said. "What a cheek!"

"But Bluebird loves trees," said Rosie, surprised.

Rosie borrowed the newspaper from Oakley and quickly looked through the pages.

"Oh, Raggles!" she said. "What have you done?"

Rosie reads the newspaper. She thinks Raggles' stories will cause trouble.

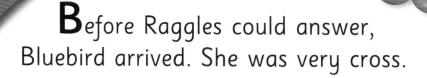

Before Raggles could answer, Bluebird arrived. She was very cross.

"I didn't say all trees were silly!" huffed Bluebird. "Just one tree."

Raggles looked confused.

Then Big Bear and Holly walked up. "Holly picked that apple as a surprise for me!" said Big Bear, in a hurt voice.

"And I was only playing football with Oakley," added Will, coming to join them. "He was in goal!"

Raggles looked down at the ground.

Read alone

Everyone is cross with Raggles.
His stories about them are not right.

Read aloud Read along

Raggles sniffed loudly. He hadn't meant to tell tales or upset anyone. He had just wanted his newspaper to be exciting.

"I'm very sorry," said Raggles, and he began to walk away, slowly.

Rosie could see Raggles was sorry for all the trouble he had caused. She followed him and put an arm around his shoulder.

Read alone

Raggles is sorry for telling tales about his friends. He didn't mean to upset them.

Read aloud   Read along

"It's okay, Raggles," said Rosie. "Your stories just need to be more cheerful ... and make people smile."

"A newspaper that makes people laugh?" wondered Raggles. "Now that's a brilliant idea!"

"Come on, then!" said Rosie. "I'll show you."

Rosie helped Raggles to write a brand new newspaper. And this time, it was full of fun!

Read alone

Rosie helps Raggles to write a brand new newspaper. The stories are much more fun!

Read aloud

Read along

The friends sat on Oakley's Hill, reading Raggles' new newspaper.

"Here's a picture of me!" pointed out Big Bear, excitedly.

"And here's a good joke," cried Will. "What did the pirate say when he dropped an anchor on his foot?"

"Ooh arrrrrr!" laughed Bluebird.

"It's the best newspaper ever," said Oakley. "Well done, Raggles."

Raggles beamed. He caught Rosie's eye and she smiled too.

Everyone likes Raggles' new newspaper.
Raggles has done well.

Read alone

Read aloud   Read along

That night, as they snuggled up in their beds, Raggles and Rosie talked about how nice it was to make their friends laugh.

"And I've got a new joke," giggled Rosie. "What do you read when you want to go to sleep … a snoozepaper!"

Raggles chuckled, and then he yawned. It had been fun being Reporter Raggles for the day!

As he dropped off to sleep Raggles thought, "I wonder what I'll be tomorrow?"

Raggles goes to bed feeling happy.
It was fun being a reporter for the day.

Sign up today!

Monthly Catchup

children's books . mags . eBooks . apps

Does your child love books?

Register for Egmont's monthly e-newsletters and access our wonderful world of characters for **FREE!**

Catchup is packed with sneak previews of new books including much-loved favourites like Mr. Men, Thomas, Ben 10, Fireman Sam and loads more. Plus you'll get **special offers, competitions** and **freebies galore.**

SIGN UP TODAY FOR EXCITING NEWS STRAIGHT TO YOUR INBOX

Head to **egmont.co.uk** to register your details (at the top of the home page) and look out for *Catchup* in your inbox.

Get a whopping 35% off your first order! So you don't miss out on special offers, freebies and prize, add this email to your address book.

Monthly Catchup

EGMONT

children's books . mags . eBooks . apps

Hello,

You haven't heard from us in a while. It's not because we've forgotten all about you! We've just been working on some brand-new ways to keep you updated about our exciting books. Once a month you can look forward to recieving our newsletter: Catchup. It'll be jam-packed with really interesting stuff like, what we've been up to, sneak previews to new books including much-loved favourites like Mr. Men, Thomas, Ben 10 and Fireman Sam, as well as news about brand-new characters and books. You'll also get updates from our magazine team, special offers, competitions and freebies galore.

Stuff to do 'n' win

Signed *Mr. Tickle* to give away...

Thomas the Tank Engine

Zhu-niverse™ here we come!

ZhuZhu Pets® have

Next month...

Sssh don't tell anyone but...

All About Bin Weevils Magazine Launching

All new special *Bin Weevils magazine,* on sale October 5th! It includes 7 amazing free gifts, comics, puzzles, posters, game tips and hints and a lot more.

All About Bin Weevils Magazine Launching

follow on Twitter | forward to a friend

So you don't miss out on special offers, freebies and prize, please add this email to your address book.

E1238